MARION COUNTY PUBLIC
321 MONROE ST.
FAIRMONT, W. VA. 26554

W9-BVA-510

# Taxi Cat
*and*
# Huey

By Gen LeRoy

Illustrated by Karen Ritz

HarperCollins*Publishers*

Taxi Cat and Huey
Copyright © 1992 by Gen LeRoy
Illustrations copyright © 1992 by Karen Ritz
All rights reserved. No part of this book may be used or reproduced in any
manner whatsoever without written permission except in the case of brief
quotations embodied in critical articles and reviews. Printed in the United
States of America. For information address HarperCollins Children's
Books, a division of HarperCollins Publishers, 10 East 53rd Street, New
York, NY 10022.
Typography by Christine Hoffman
1 2 3 4 5 6 7 8 9 10
First Edition

Library of Congress Cataloging-in-Publication Data
LeRoy, Gen.
    Taxi cat and Huey / by Gen LeRoy : illustrated by Karen Ritz.
        p.      cm.
    Summary: A basset hound's peaceful life with a human couple is
changed when a rambunctious and adventurous cat joins the family.
    ISBN 0-06-021768-5. — ISBN 0-06-021769-3 (lib.bdg.)
    [1. Dogs—Fiction.  2. Cats—Fiction.  3. Humorous stories.]
I. Ritz, Karen, ill.  II. Title.
PZ7.L5615Tax 1992                                              90-27383
[Fic]—dc20                                                          CIP
                                                                     AC

*For Georgia Freed,*
*with special love*
*—G.L.*

*With thanks to*
*Sandy Hardy*
*—K.R.*

# 1

I'd better start at the beginning of my story.
My name is Huey, short for Hubert. I'm six
years old and I live in New York City with
Fred and Maureen Walton.

I have stubby legs, a longish body, an
extremely large and sensitive nose, and very
droopy eyes that always look sad.

I'm a basset hound.

Up until a year ago I lived here with my
mother, Grace. Then, one morning, I woke up
but she didn't. The Waltons cried and cried.
She had been their first dog. They drove out
to the country, buried her under a tree, put
up a wooden marker with her name on it,
boo-hooed some more, then turned around
and headed back to the city. When we got
home, they packed away her cushion and fed
me Liver Treats for over a week.

I did miss her a lot.

And I did feel a little blue being left home on my own all day while the Waltons went off to work. But . . . that is *still* no excuse for what happened next.

"Huey? Look. We've brought you home a pet, a little playmate to keep you company," Maureen said. She was all excited.

They put the box down in front of me. I took one sniff and nearly died. CAT! The smell was absolutely *disgusting!*

I peered over the edge of the box and found myself nose to nose with a crazy-looking cross-eyed cat. Suddenly, without any warning, its paw thwacked me right across my sensitive nose and I nearly hit the ceiling. I let out a *HOWL* and *zip!* I was out of there!

"It's only a kitten, Huey. We're calling him Taxi. Come out from under there. Don't act like that."

She tried to reach for me under the sofa, but I pressed closer to the wall.

"We got him from the pound. They were going to put him to sleep. Come out, Huey. I can't stay down here on my knees all night. Please? Cats are wonderful company. They're independent, quiet, undemanding. Fascinating to

2

watch. You'll see. Now, come on out. How will you ever get to know him from under there?"

She had the nerve to drag me out by my back legs! How undignified.

Then she carried me into the kitchen to take another look at that nasty little cat whose crossed eyes were trying to focus on a winter fly doing some loop-de-loops.

"Taxi's food and water will be on that side of the kitchen and yours will stay on this side. His litter box is by the back door."

So what?

I couldn't care less.

I wriggled out of her arms and slid to the floor. That cat was not going to get its filthy paws on any of my things.

No sir.

I found my favorite bone and stuck it under my bed. Then I searched around for my push-me-pull-you toy, my ball with the bell inside, my cookies, my rawhide Big Boy Bone, and my baseball hat and piled them on top of my bed.

There.

If he dared to come anywhere near my things, I'd make him wish he'd never set foot in my apartment.

I crept back into the kitchen and saw something at the far end of the room. It was a long, thin leather strap with a knot tied at one end. I wasn't sure what it was exactly and was about to give it a sniff when I heard an awful kind of hissing sound behind me. I spun around just in time to see that insane cat *diving* at me, teeth first!

I dropped the string and flew out of the room.

"Huey? You mustn't act this way. That piece of string belongs to Taxi. It's special to him. Like a pet. He doesn't like anyone to touch it. You understand. Come out from under there."

The cat was a menace to society!

I was not going to come out from under that cabinet until *he* went away.

So I waited.

And waited.

But, no one came looking for me, so finally I strolled into the kitchen. And there, believe it or not, was that cat eating with his wretched string dipped into the food bowl next to him. He finished and dunked the

string into the water bowl while he took a drink. Then he dragged the string into the litter box for a moment, then pulled it to the middle of the floor and started jumping up and down on it. Giving it punches. Flinging it into the air, catching it in his teeth, then shaking it.

He carried on like that until he tired himself out. Then he took his ratty-looking string over to his cushion and fell asleep. *Thunk.* Just like that.

That cat was a mental case. A total fruitcake! The Waltons, in all their innocence, had brought me home an unwanted animal with a toasted marshmallow for a brain.

How could they think that I would have any interest in making friends with an animal who thought a piece of knotted leather string was his pet!

Basset hounds have their pride, you know. We're a dignified breed. All the way from England.

I went into the living room but didn't feel like watching television with the Waltons. I much preferred to sulk.

And . . . so I did.

# 2

Even though I kept my distance, I still couldn't help but notice some disturbing habits that cat had.

One of them was sleeping.

After the first night, he never bothered with the cushion. No. He took to sleeping draped over doors. Now, this may seem cute to you, but it isn't. Have you ever walked from, say, the living room into the kitchen when suddenly *plop*, a cat fell on your head?

That's exactly what happened, and I can tell you it is a grisly experience.

He also liked hanging down from the chandelier.

That was fine until someone turned on the light!

Then the cat would let out a *screech*, *ping* straight up, then crash-land on the floor. Graceful? Not this cat. This cat was a fur-covered disaster area. The most accident-prone cat I ever laid eyes on.

And talk about repulsive habits!

He ate bugs.

Filthy creepy-crawlies, which he devoured with glee. Moths. Flies. Cockroaches. Yes . . . *cockroaches!* Crunching away on them until I thought I'd go mad.

*Chomp! Chomp! Crunch!* Swallow.

Can you believe it?

Another miserable habit he had often made my heart stop beating altogether. There he would be. His slitty crossed eyes nearly closing, as though he were about to snooze, when suddenly he'd look up in stark terror as if some monster had clumped into the room. *Wham!* He'd leap straight up into the air.

*Boing!*

And with his hair sticking out all over the place and his tail swelled up as if someone had pumped it up with an air hose, he'd go bounding from room to room, completely freaked out!

*Boing! Boing! Booooiing!*

On one of these weird hopping sprees, he accidentally boinged onto the TV remote control. All of a sudden a voice *boomed* into the room: "GET YOUR FREE GIFT NOW, RUN, RUN, DON'T WALK, DOWN TO McDOUGAL'S WAREHOUSE. . . ."

We lit out of the room like two streaks of lightning.

After a while we crept back into the room. Taxi cautiously approached the TV remote control again. Gave it a poke. Watched as the channels changed and stopped poking when it got to a station showing cartoons.

It was *Tom and Jerry.*

He liked it.

He picked up his string, settled on the sofa in front of the TV set, and watched while I stayed half hidden behind the sofa, listening to the rain outside. Suddenly from way down below on the street, I could hear someone calling.

"TAXXIIII!"

Taxi stood straight up with his string in his mouth and looked around, trying to figure out who was calling him.

"TAAAXXI! *TAAAAXIII!*"

He hopped onto the windowsill and looked this way and that. Suddenly we could hear another voice calling from the other side of the room.

"TAAAXXIIII! OVER *HERE!* WHOA! *TAXI!*"

He leaped each time his name was called and dashed around, leaping on and off windowsills, doing nosedives as he skidded out of the room.

I couldn't help laughing.

I mean, there they were, Tom and Jerry on TV chasing each other around, crashing into things, and here, right here in my own living room, the very same thing was happening.

I was howling so loud that I didn't even hear the Waltons come in the door.

"Who turned on the TV?" was their first question. Their second was:

"Where's Taxi?"

I shrugged. I knew what was coming next.

"TAXXIII! *TAAAAAXX*III, where are you?"

"Huey? Help. Come on. Where is he?"

I knew they'd eventually come to me for help. Anything that's lost I generally can find.

It's the nose.

The nose is legendary.

I cocked my head, took a looooong sniff, and smiled to myself. That cat would be a cinch to find. Fear and panic really stink.

I went from room to room with my nose to the floor, sniffing away. I wanted to draw out the suspense a little longer.

Once in a while I'd raise my head and let out a "*WHOOOOOooo OOOooo OOoo!*" Just for dramatic effect.

When I thought the Waltons couldn't stand it any longer, I led them to the place where I knew Taxi was hiding all the while. A back, back closet, stuck inside the bottom of a moldy old golf bag. When I say stuck, I mean stuck.

They had to *slice* that cat out of the bag. And when they finally lifted him out, his eyes were aglow with stark terror and he was covered all over with moldy little green bits. Maureen had the bright idea of trying to clean him off with her brand-new Dustbuster.

Well, forget it.

That cat squirmed around like a snake with a big itch, trying to get away.

Quiet? Independent? Fascinating to watch? Ha! He was nothing but trouble from the day he arrived.

"Come on, Huey. Walk time," called Maureen

when they gave up vacuuming the cat.

I must say I needed a breath of fresh air.

Maureen hooked my leash to my collar, pulled some plastic sandwich bags over my ears, then helped me step into four more plastic Baggies, which she fastened with rubber bands. This was something we always did when it rained. My ears tend to drag through every puddle on the street.

As Fred and I were heading for the door, I heard some peculiar squeaky noise behind me and turned to see that wicked cat laughing at me. Not only that, but he was holding up that ridiculous tattered string so *it* could take a look at me too!

I was mortified!

I yanked Fred out the open door and raced toward the elevator. So what if I had to wear plastic Baggies on my ears and feet. It was better than dragging half of New York City's slime back inside the apartment.

How *dare* that cat laugh at me? I was *never* going to befriend him now.

Never!

# 3

Well, this is a real example of how your strongest convictions can go astray. There I was, fed up—ready to pack up my bones and run away—when a most peculiar thing happened that sort of turned everything around.

It was just an ordinary day, like all the others, when suddenly I heard a strange noise at the back door.

I went to investigate.

Someone was trying to break in! This had never happened before, so I didn't exactly know what to do. I watched as the brand-new locks *splintered* from the door and clunked to the floor. The chain was clipped with some nasty-looking shears, and in walked two strangers. Men. One of them was carrying a sack. The other a crowbar. I gave each of them a bark.

"Beat it!" one of them growled, and being an

obedient dog, I dove right under the kitchen sink. As they passed by, I took a long sniff. I could smell fear and anger.

After a moment I arose and followed at a safe distance as they found their way into the living room.

Taxi didn't appear to notice them. He was engrossed in his life-and-death battle with a moth.

What a useless creature.

Then a sudden thought struck me. Wouldn't it be wonderful if they stole the cat?

I hoped they'd notice him sitting under the lamp—his dark fur slick and shiny, his narrow green eyes glinting in the light. So what if they were crossed? His strong jaws . . . mashing the moth.

But the men seemed more interested in disconnecting the television, the stereo, the VCR, and the silver wall sconces.

Maureen was going to be very upset. Those sconces had belonged to her grandmother.

Fred was going to be upset too. The men took his good camera.

They didn't even notice Taxi.

Finally their sack was stuffed.

"Tie it up," one of them ordered the other.

"With what?"

"That." He pointed at Taxi's string.

As the man went to grab the string, Taxi's front leg suddenly reached out and clamped a sturdy claw onto it, anchoring the string to the table.

"Leggo!" The man swiped at Taxi and tried to yank the string free.

All of a sudden, Taxi let out this hair-raising SCREECH, just like something out of a jungle film, and with claws protruding and teeth flashing, he attacked.

The man yelled with pain as he raced around the room, twisting and turning and trying to unprong Taxi from his back.

When the other man tried to help, Taxi jumped straight at him and started scratching. The man fell onto the side table, knocking it over and spilling everything to the floor.

Up the drapery Taxi ran, across the molding at the top, to make an aerial assault on the two crooks.

It seemed as if there were fifty cats inside that room.

Finally the men ran for the back door, one of

them with a crazed cat attached to his butt.

I could hear some cussing, a thud, a tumble, and then everything went quiet.

I stayed under the sofa and waited.

Just when I was beginning to get a little worried, Taxi strutted into the room, hopped onto the back of the sofa, and let out a yell that could have awakened the dead.

"NINNNNJAAAAA!"

Then he flipped backward off the sofa and did a few somersaults, some sideways flips, and a little jogging, until he wore himself out and leaned against the wall, panting.

I crept out from under the sofa.

"That was really something," I said, breaking my solemn oath not to speak to him.

He cocked his head to one side and stared at me.

"My name is Huey," I said.

His eyes narrowed in a peculiar way. Maybe he didn't understand English. Maybe he was a foreign cat.

"You from . . . away? Away? Your country . . . away?"

He jumped down off his perch and slunk over to me, pressing his nose against mine.

"Listen, Lardnose. I don't know what your problem is but you're looking at *Ninja*. Get it? I am a ninja warrior."

Then he spun around, flexed his muscles, and made an impossible leap for the mantelpiece, stopping midway to catch a fly between his teeth. He missed the mantel and landed in the azalea plant.

I didn't say a word.

He mumbled to himself as he stepped out of the pot. He found his string and began to groom it and then himself.

It was definitely cuckootime on Central Park West.

I sat and watched. Finally he looked straight at me.

"Anyone messes with my snake and they're dead. You get me? D-E-A-D. Dead."

"Snake?" I asked, looking at the limp string.

Instantly, we were nose to nose.

"Yes. Snake! What did you think it was, Porkhead?"

"Wellll . . . in my utter stupidity, I thought it resembled a piece of string. With a knot tied at one end."

"Well, you're wrong! His name is Sushi. He's my very own personal, private assistant."

He moved away and I swallowed.

"My ancestors were bred in palaces. Their job was to protect kings and queens. We were trained to perch on their shoulders and . . . if we sensed danger approaching, we would *leap* onto the enemy and *rip out his throat!*"

I swallowed hard. Wow!

He let out a yell, swung around, and gave the curtain a swat. Then he spun around real fast to make sure I wasn't sneaking up on him.

"What! Did you hear that?" he asked. Someone was coming down the corridor. "It's those burglars," Taxi said, "coming back for their loot. HA! Will *they* have a surprise."

"Wait, Taxi . . . no . . ."

"Quiet!" he warned.

I knew what was about to happen, so I crept way under the sofa and hid.

As the door opened, Taxi let out one of his freaky screeches and went sailing across the room. I could hear lots of screams and commotion as the lights came on.

"What in the world's happened in here?" Maureen cried.

She and Fred stood in the doorway, open-mouthed, their groceries scattered on the floor. They stared at the mess left behind by the burglars, including the sack in the middle of the room with all their things inside.

Above their heads, clinging to the ceiling fixture, was Taxi, looking very sheepish.

# 4
---

"How could they possibly think it was you who scared away those thieves? Huey the Watchdog? Ha!"

It was a few weeks later, but Taxi was still on at me about that day.

"Look at you. For one thing, your legs are too short. You need another pair just to hold up that stomach of yours. You couldn't scare away a tick."

"I offered you a share of my Liver Treats, didn't I?"

"Phooey! Ninja warriors hate Liver Treats."

"And my Sausage Bits."

"Double yuck."

He gave me a poke in my ribs.

"No wonder you're so fat, Huey. You eat all that junk. Even when you're resting you're gnawing on a bone. Look at you. Your head's too big. You've got those awful bags under your eyes, and your eyeballs look like under-done steak. Flab. Flab. Flab."

"I'll have you know I am a perfect example of a typical basset hound."

"You're not built for speed, Huey. Or beauty. Or anything. That's why you're such a coward. You can't move around corners."

"Coward!" How dare he?

A fly suddenly swooped in front of him, breaking his concentration. As he leaped for it, I ducked out of the room.

Calling me a coward!

He was such a bully!

He had forced me to eat a cockroach a few days earlier. Said it was all protein and how could I consider myself worldly if I didn't try different kinds of foods?

I tried it.

It was positively *dees-gusting!*

"Huey?"

Maureen was there with my leash. She attached it to my collar. This was unusual. It wasn't my walk time.

Fred had put Taxi inside his traveling box.

"Where are we going?" he asked me in the elevator.

"I don't know," I answered.

We were put into the back of the station wagon. "Maybe to the park?" I said.

Taxi was getting excited. "This'll be interesting. I always wanted to take a look at the park. Maybe I'll show you how to climb a tree or two."

"Dogs cannot climb trees."

"You can if you lose a few pounds of that flab."

The station wagon drove past the park.

"Hey. Wasn't that the park? Where're we going?" Taxi asked again.

"Maybe to the groomers," I said.

"Groomers?" He laughed. "You've got to be kidding. Cats don't go to groomers. We take care of ourselves. Look at this face. These whiskers. These teeth. Perfect!"

I peered out the window.

"We passed the groomers," I said. I was beginning to worry. "I wish I could figure out just where we're going. I don't like driving around not knowing."

"Don't be such a wimp," Taxi said. "It'll be an adventure, whatever it is. Anything's better than sitting in that apartment all day."

"Maybe we're going to visit their friends."

"I hope they have cockroaches there. They're getting a little scarce back at the apartment."

"Yes, but these friends unfortunately have a little boy who likes to pull my tail."

"I'll take care of him. Will you stop worrying, Huey? You worry about everything. No wonder you look like such a mess. Sit back. Relax."

I tried.

But, I couldn't.

We drove right past their friends' apartment building and turned onto a wider street.

Then, after another block or so, the station wagon pulled into a parking space and stopped.

Now I knew where we were.

"We're going to the vet's office," I said. Well! Taxi's eyes grew as big as saucers and he started to quiver and shake.

"The *what* office? You have to be KIDDING! *LET ME OUTTA HERE!*"

He started to carry on like a lunatic. Rattling the bars of his box. Screaming his head off. You would've thought someone was trying to kill that cat.

I tried to calm him down, but . . . forget it!

"HELP! *MURDER!* SOMEBODY HELLLP!" he screamed.

It was *SOO*ooo embarrassing.

In fact, I walked a little ahead so people wouldn't think I knew him.

As soon as we entered the office, the nurse ushered us into a room. The vet showed up a moment later.

"Hello, Huey." He patted me on the head and then turned to study the cringing cat, pressed into a back corner of his box.

"Well. And who do we have here?"

"NOOOO! GET AWAY! HUEY? HELP ME! BITE HIM! PEE ON HIM! SIC HIM! KILL!"

They tried to get him out of the box, but Taxi's claws were pronged to the wicker side.

"I'm going to *throw up on you!* I *am!* STOP IT!"

Finally they got him out.

And Taxi sprang into action.

That cat seemed to be everywhere at once. Hopping all over the place like some Mexican jumping bean gone wrong. Every time it

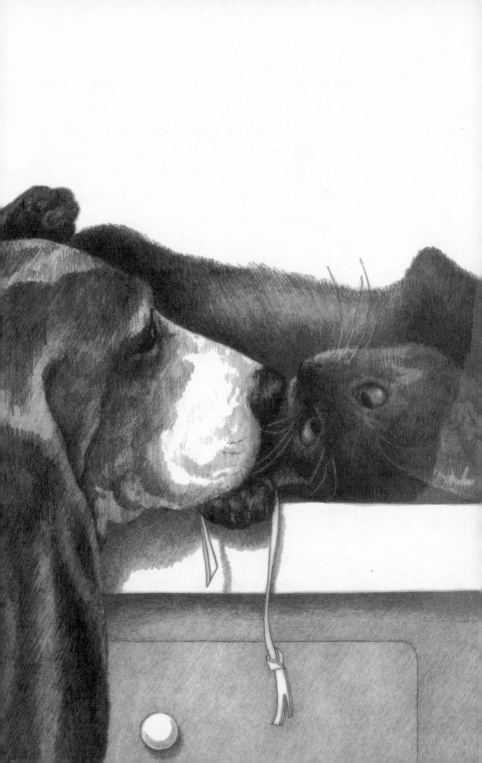

looked as if someone might catch him, off he would go, crashing into rows of medicine bottles and spilling them to the floor, knocking over a bookcase that scattered magazines and x-ray files all over the place.

I stayed out of everyone's way by ducking under the desk. Waiting for things to calm down.

Finally they managed to subdue him, and the vet gave him an injection to quiet him down.

"I AM NINNNNJA WARRIOR! I DIE NINJAAA! . . . Ouch! Hey. That hurt."

He staggered around for a minute, then collapsed with one of his paws outstretched in my direction.

"Take . . . care . . . of . . . Sushi," he said, then coughed, hiccupped, and fell into a deep sleep.

Honest, now. How dramatic could you get?

"I'm so sorry," Maureen said. I could tell the vet was upset as he tried, with his assistants, to clean things up.

"He's an exotic mixture. Part Siamese and who knows what else," Fred said, picking up the magazines scattered on the floor. "He's very high-strung."

You could say *that* again!

The vet began to examine Taxi.

"Very strong," the vet commented. "You say you got him from the pound?"

"Yes," Maureen responded. "He was the only one of the litter that survived."

My ears perked up.

"Some children found him clinging to a rock in the middle of a stream. He had that leather string he carries in his mouth. We think it may've been the one that was tied around the bag that held the rest of the litter."

I was amazed.

"One of the people down at the pound said that, strange as this may sound, he thought Taxi had tried to save the others by loosening the string and opening the bag. But the current swept the bag downriver, and the others drowned," said Fred.

"He won't be parted from that string," Maureen added.

I looked down at Sushi.

Then up at Taxi asleep on the table.

I felt that I understood him a little better now.

And I decided that from now on I would try to be kinder to him.

# 5

"Okay, Huey, I want the truth."

For weeks afterward that cat pestered the life out of me. This time he had me trapped under a bench.

"Do I have an incurable disease?"

"No, Taxi."

"Did the vet pull something out while I was asleep?"

"No, Taxi."

"Am I missing a lung? A kidney? Is my stomach filled with warts?"

"No, Taxi."

"Then *why* are you being so *nice* to me?"

He let me out, and I skidded down the hallway and nearly bonked into a large crate that Maureen and Fred were carrying out of their bedroom.

They had taken down all the books and pictures and had packed them into boxes and crates. The place was a mess. And disorder always makes me feel a little jumpy. I'd put my bone one place, and an hour later it had been moved somewhere else. With all this commotion I was relieved to go out for a walk. But do you think that cat could let me have a little peace?

Fat chance!

I would hear "YOOOOO-HOOOOooo" all the way down from the narrow ledge where he was standing eight floors up.

Anything for attention!

I guess he wanted to show me he wasn't a coward for acting the way he had inside the vet's office. Not that I ever made fun of him. I'm not like that. But then, I suppose he thought I didn't make fun of him because he was dying of some incurable disease or had a belly full of warts.

All I was concerned about was Taxi falling off the ledge and *splat* . . . becoming a piece of street pizza. That's what you call squirrels and birds and other animals that get squished by trucks or cars. Or fall off eight-story buildings.

Anyway, the packing continued until a few

days later when we were taken down to the station wagon. And Taxi freaked for a moment until it became clear that we were not headed back to the vet's office. Then he quieted down.

We drove through the city, passing tall buildings, whizzing past clumps of people standing on corners. Down a long, wide street, dwarfed by busses and trucks. I couldn't tell where we were until we finally drove across a bridge and I was able to see the city, now far behind us.

The sound of the wheels against the highway put me to sleep. When I awoke, we were traveling along a highway with nothing but fields on either side.

"I thought you'd never wake up," Taxi said to me from inside his box. He was trying to see out the window too.

I sniffed the air.

"Well?" he asked, a little anxious.

"Something smells a little familiar, but I can't tell what it is."

After a while we turned off the highway and onto a country road. The traffic thinned. The trees became denser on both sides. The landscape was dotted with farms and ponds and patchworked with cornfields and potato fields.

"This is somewhere near where my mother is buried," I exclaimed. Now smells were much more familiar.

"We're going to a *cemetery*!"

"No. We're going to the countryside."

"Why?"

"Fresh air, I suppose. Why else? And from the amount of stuff they brought, I bet we'll stay for a while."

"I don't trust them. They're up to something."

"The Waltons? How could you say that, Taxi? They are the kindest, most generous people in the whole wide world."

"Believe what you will. Ninja trusts no one."

"Oh. Ninja schminja."

"Maybe they're going to have us stuffed so they won't have to feed us any longer. Wellll . . . they won't take *me* without a fight."

"Have you lost your marbles, Taxi?"

"Believe what you will. Ninja will wait and watch."

I ignored him.

He was in one of his moods. Looking suspiciously at everything. Making up horrible plans inside his warped brain.

After a long while we pulled into a tree-lined driveway that led to a small house set on the banks of a gentle bay.

There were plenty of trees. Plenty of bushes. Lots of tall marsh grass.

I was in heaven.

As soon as they opened the car door, I hopped out to take a look around.

"Hey! Lemme outta this box, will you?" Taxi called behind me.

But Fred carried him locked inside his box into the house, then came out and, bit by bit, unloaded the car with Maureen.

There were so many smells in the air.

Raccoon. Rabbit. Squirrels. Birds. Cats. Dogs. Horses. Cows. And fish.

Every breeze brought with it another new and tantalizing aroma, evoking all sorts of exciting pictures inside my mind.

"LEMME OUTTA HERE, ya big BABOON!" Taxi was sitting in his box, inside the house, screaming his head off.

Maureen finally undid the latch on his traveling box.

"Now stay indoors, Taxi."

But no sooner did she have the door opened than Taxi shot past her outstretched hands, flew outside, and ran straight up the first tree he came to.

Maureen and Fred stood at the bottom and tried to coax him down.

"Taxi? Please come down," they both purred.

"No way, José," he mewed. "Get lost."

"Taxi!" I called."They won't let you out again if you behave like this. Come down this second."

"Go stick your nose in an eggbeater. I'm not budging."

"Taxi? We have some nice Gourmet Fish Surprise for you. Come down, won't you?"

"Gourmet Fish Surprise?" he mocked. "Out of a can? What do you expect me to do, swoon?"

He climbed even higher. So high that I could barely see him. He slipped out onto the far end of a limb, which bent under his weight.

Fred and Maureen were worried he might fall off and began hunting for a ladder. I felt just awful that he was causing them so much trouble their first day there.

"Just show them you can get down, Taxi. Then they'll stop worrying."

"I'll come down when I'm ready. I don't need them coddling me like some overstuffed dog. My ancestors lived outdoors. Why can't I?"

"Because it could rain on you."

"So? I'll get under some leaves."

"Suppose a huge eagle with giant talons swoops out of the sky? He'll gobble you up and spit out the bones sooner than you . . ."

Before I could finish, Taxi sprinted down the tree and practically *flew* into the house, almost knocking over Maureen and Fred, who had found a small rickety ladder.

They just stood there looking quite confused.

So. Ninja the Great was afraid of eagles, was he?

"Lock the door, honey," Maureen said. "Make sure everything's closed up for the night. I don't want to lose the cat."

Didn't she realize that nothing was going to keep a cat like Taxi from going where he had a mind to go or doing anything other than what pleased him?

# 6

It didn't take them long to get the picture.

They'd close Taxi inside the house and head out on a raft, and just before they'd begin sunning themselves, one of them would look back and see Taxi outside.

Or they'd come home from shopping and there Taxi would be, hanging over the edge of the roof, dangling his string.

"Hi, y'all," he'd say, and slap at their hair as they passed beneath him, shaking their heads in astonishment.

"How in the world does he manage to get out?"

"I *know* I locked the door," Fred would add.

Finally they gave up and allowed Taxi freedom to come and go as he pleased. He always came back, and that was the only thing they cared about.

As for me, he had started out being *my* pet

and somehow or other I was ending up being *his* pet.

"Huey, wake up. Come on. I need some help."

I opened one eye and peered up at him.

"It's the middle of the night, Taxi. If you need help, ask Sushi. Isn't he your assistant?"

"Come on. You sleep *too* much, Blimpo. Life is passing you by!"

He gave me a poke. I rolled over and yawned.

"Come on." He nipped at my feet, at my ears, pushed and prodded until I was out the door.

"Down those steps. To the right. Over there. NO! There!"

"Don't twist my nose like that. It's not a steering wheel, you know."

"See the rope? There."

"You brought me out here to see a *rope*?"

"Undo the knot."

"Why?"

"Just undo it, Huey. Use your teeth. That's it. Harder. Move onto the wooden bit—you can get to it easier."

I gnawed at the rope until the knot came undone.

Immediately I felt us moving.

"Hey . . . we're . . . *moving*! *JUMP*!"

"No! Whoa, Huey. This is what I got you up for. We're going to have ourselves a little adventure."

"This is *not* a little adventure. It's a little *RAFT*!"

"Relax. There's nothing to it," Taxi insisted, as I tried to jump off. "I've been watching the Waltons. They get on. The raft glides over to the other side of the bay, and then it goes right back to where it started from."

"The raft doesn't do it on its *own*, Taxi," I explained as calmly as my hysterical mind would allow. "The Waltons use paddles! That's how they steer this thing!"

"Paddles?" Taxi looked a little vague. "You mean those long sticks of wood?"

"Yes, Taxi." I looked back at the shore moving farther away from us. "We're heading straight out to sea! What'll we do? You can't swim and I don't think your snake'll float! WOOOOoooo. WOOOOoooo." I started to call for help.

"Stop yapping. Look. There's a strip of land just over there. You can swim to it and I'll ride on your back."

"That's a SANDBAR, Taxi. A sandbar gets *covered* with water at high tide!"

"Oh" was all he said.

I started shoving and wriggling, trying to move the raft to the opposite bank.

It was hard. We were going against the tide.

Why, oh why, had I listened to that cat? Life used to be so calm and peaceful before he came along. And now there I was in the middle of a tidal wave, moments away from drowning.

"Quick! Jump," he ordered.

Before I knew what happened, he shoved me into the cold, cold water and was standing on my back.

I wasn't convinced I could swim. When would I have had an opportunity to try it?

It was hard work, I can tell you. Between the weight of my soaking wet ears pulling me down and Taxi riding on my shoulders, I had to swim like the dickens to keep my own head above water.

"Over there. To the left," he commanded.

I headed straight for a long, low jetty that jutted out from the opposite shore.

How he could direct us in the dark, I'll never know.

It was luck. Pure luck.

We climbed onto the jetty and watched the raft go swirling away toward the mouth of the bay, beyond which lay the open sea.

"How're we going to get back?" I asked. A little worried.

But Taxi wasn't. He was lying on the ground, looking up at the sky.

"Look at all those stars," he said.

"They are the same stars we saw from the other side of the bay," I reminded him. "How are we *ever* going to get back?"

"Will you stop yapping and enjoy yourself? Don't you have any adventure in your soul, Huey? Do you only want to wake up, get fed, and go to sleep your whole life long?"

I hadn't regarded my life in that manner. But I guess that's about all I had been doing. It became very clear just then that Taxi's life had been extremely interesting, while mine had been rather uneventful.

"Let's look this place over," he said, rising. "Nothing's going to happen to you. Not while you have Sushi and me to protect you."

Somehow, keeping company with a deranged cat and a piece of chewed-up leather string did not make me feel all that secure. But I hid my anxieties and decided to try and have a good time.

We climbed up a small rise. It was a beautiful night. The stars sparkled in the black sky. The moon beamed like a white smile. We stood on the crest, gazing up, when we heard from behind us . . .

"Moooooo."

Taxi spun around. A cow was standing not five feet away. And beyond him was a long, wide meadow with other cows silhouetted in the moonlight.

"A *cow*!" Taxi got very excited. "A real *COW*!" And off he flew, taking Sushi with him.

I tried to follow but lost him in the dark. Then I heard:

"Look at me!"

I climbed onto a stack of wood and saw Taxi standing on the back of one of the cows.

"Giddy-up!" he shouted.

Something wasn't right.

I mean, something looked all wrong.

"I got a dud cow here," Taxi called out as he leaped onto another cow's back.

Then I saw what it was. Cows don't wear rings through their noses. But *bulls* do!

"Taxi . . . wait . . . don't."

The one Taxi was on pawed the ground, then began to buck, toss, rear back, and do all sorts of contortions. Anything to get that cat off.

Taxi held on like a true rodeo rider. He whooped and hollered and scared the living daylights out of all the rest of the cattle and bulls and whatever else was inside that corral. Before long that crazy cat started a *stampede*!

Lights lit up inside a nearby house, the occupants awakened by the noise.

A couple of men jumped into a Jeep to head off the animals.

Over all the commotion and the shouting, dust flying, hooves pounding, I thought I could hear a faint . . .

"Niiiiinnnnnjaaa!"

But I couldn't be too sure.

Why had I listened to him? He was probably dead somewhere by now. Smeared on the

ground like a slice of street pizza, and some-how I felt very responsible.

After all, he *was* my pet.

I shuddered at the thought of how upset Maureen and Fred would be.

I waited and waited until the moon started to drop closer to the bay, and then I began to search for Taxi. No matter how I covered the area, I couldn't find him. No matter how much I sniffed, I couldn't pick up the faintest scent.

The tide was too high and the current looked too strong. I was frightened of trying to swim it on my own, so I turned toward a long pathway that I hoped would lead me around the bay and back to the Waltons.

Maybe I could get them to come back and help me find that idiotic cat.

# 7

It was two o'clock the next afternoon when the police car stopped next to me on the side of the road. I had become hopelessly lost in the night. The path I had started on twisted and turned and led me far away from the bay. Every other path I tried led me nowhere.

I hadn't slept one wink worrying about that cat.

I was a total nervous wreck and was covered with burrs and ticks and possibly fleas.

I barked, trying to make the police follow me back. Back to the pasture so they could help me find Taxi. But they didn't understand. They checked my collar, then slung me into their car and drove me back to the Waltons.

Maureen and Fred were so pleased to see me that it made me feel worse. They wanted to feed me, brush me, and I don't know what

else. While all I wanted was for them to follow me back to the pasture.

I barked and backed out the door, then charged at them, barking and backing for the door again. But they didn't catch on.

I would have to get back across the bay at night to look for Taxi myself.

I was all mixed up. And tired. I didn't know what to do. I couldn't remember ever feeling such a loss, except, of course, right after my mother died. I was actually missing that lunatic cat.

Maureen tried to force some Liver Treats on me, but how could I possibly eat when Taxi was probably pinned under some bull's hoof, crying out for help?

I trundled into the living room to peer out the window. My heart felt so heavy. And then it stopped.

*Guess* who was curled up on the sofa, watching a Bugs Bunny cartoon!

That's right. Taxi!

I didn't know whether to bite him or kiss him. I was happy *and* raging mad at the same time. I could feel the blood bubbling up inside my head.

"*How* . . . did you *GET* here?" was all I could say.

"A piece of cake," he answered, and winked at me.

I stood staring at him.

"I've got *three ticks* on your account!"

"Ticks? I love ticks. They're a little hard at first, but they're *very* tasty. Where are they?"

"I thought you were dead."

"Me?" He stood up. "Haven't you heard? A cat's got nine lives, and I've only used up about one and a half of my lifetime supply."

Maureen entered and stroked Taxi's back.

Not liking to be stroked, he retreated. Maureen moved closer to me and began scratching my ears.

"I was worried about you, Huey. It's so unlike you to go wandering off. It's a good thing you have a collar."

Fred came in and handed me a biscuit, which I tried to go off and hide, but Maureen held on to my back legs.

"So that nothing happens to you, Huey, we're going to tie you up for a while. Just at night, so you don't wander off," Fred said.

Tie ME up? I was flabbergasted.

"Tsk, tsk," Taxi taunted. "Naughty doggie. Naughty, naughty boy."

I wanted to strangle him.

"This is *your* fault, you wretch! You dragged me off on that stupid adventure!"

Fred hooked the leash on me, then hitched the end to a rope, which he looped onto the clothesline out back.

I sat at the edge of the porch in a complete snit. I wouldn't look at any of them. When they gave me a dish of water, I nudged it away with my nose.

I wanted them to see how degraded I felt. A basset hound. Tied to a *leash!*

Eventually, they went to bed.

The moon was rising. Its smile was wider than the night before. More of a laugh than a grin. It was probably laughing at me.

Taxi slid outside and plonked down beside me. I didn't turn. I was finished with that miserable cat.

Fifty stampeding bulls! Couldn't at least *one* of them have stepped on him?

"Wanna see what's happening in town tonight?"

"Get lost," I answered. He climbed a tree

and stared down at me from the lowest branch.

"So one of our adventures turned a little sour. So what? That doesn't mean it'll happen with all the others. Come on. Let's go check out the neighbors."

"I am tied to a clothesline. Remember?"

"Tied schmied. That's nothing."

"I don't want to have anything more to do with you. . . ."

I smelled the raccoons before I could see them. They were on the side of the house. Trying to get the lid off the garbage can. Another long sniff and I could tell they were adults. Male.

I started around the side. But before I got halfway there, the rope got caught around the porch furniture. I tried to backtrack hoping to untangle myself, but only managed to make matters worse.

"Get *away* from that GARBAGE!" I yelled, trying to sound fierce.

Suddenly there they were, peering at me from around the side of the house. Like two masked bandits.

"Shoo," I said.

They advanced. I retreated. But not too far. I was caught by the rope. I backed up against the house as they drew closer.

"Leave him alone, fellas," Taxi said in a very relaxed voice.

One of them glanced up at Taxi.

"Beat it," Taxi snarled.

But they came closer. Ready to attack.

"I said . . . don't go near that dog." This time he used a different voice. A voice I remembered hearing once before. Uh-oh, I thought to myself.

They didn't even bother to look at him. Their eyes gleamed in the night. Wicked smiles curled back their lips as they came toward me.

Then:

"NINNNNNNJAAAAA!"

All they were able to see was a ball of fur flying at them as Taxi went into the most spectacular acrobatics I had ever seen.

Scratching, biting, kicking, and I don't know what else.

In minutes he drove them off the porch and toward the water.

The growling and wailing were *awesome*.

A light went on inside the house and both Fred and Maureen ran outside.

"Oh, Huey," they said, bending down near me. "You've almost strangled yourself." They untwisted the rope, then unlatched the leash and patted me on the back.

"Poor Huey. We'd better forget about this idea. You old thing, you. You shouldn't be tied up now, should you? It isn't at all dignified, is it?"

"Absolutely not," I agreed. Only it came out as a pathetic howl. They both laughed.

"Taxi. Come out of those bushes."

He did.

"Don't run off and leave Huey like this. You ought to take care of him."

Taxi looked at them as if they had each sprouted another head. And kept looking at them as they went back inside and shut the door.

"Humans can be SOOoooo dense," he said.

They had the whole thing back to front. I looked at Taxi. His eyes were shining in the moonlight.

"Thanks."

"Forget it," he said. Then he came over and

sat next to me.

"Tomorrow, we check out the town, okay?"

I wasn't too sure.

Taxi stretched his forequarters, then his hind legs, and became this long, skinny cat. Then he arched his back real high and became an inverted letter "U." He yawned and blinked my way.

"You'll come," he said with a grin filled with confidence.

# 8

Taxi was halfway up the path by the time I reached him.

"Where are we going?"

"Who knows? If you want something to happen, Huey, you have to invent it yourself. Curiosity never killed a cat, and that's why we have more fun than dogs do."

"Dogs have fun."

"No, they don't. You *need* people to play with you. Do you ever see cats tripping over their tongues to go fetch a ball? No. Did you ever see any of my species jumping into an ice-cold pond to drag out a dirty piece of splintering wood only so that some dumbo can fling it back again? Of course not. We aren't stupid. And did you ever once see me beg and *begggg* to have someone play with me? Never. I need no one. I'm imaginative. I have a GREAT mind."

"Dogs don't have nine lives."

"So? Do you want to spend the only one you have sitting on your fat keister waiting for someone to tell you what to do with your time? You have to go out and meet this world halfway."

We were heading along the road that led into town.

"Don't be worried," he added, as though he were reading my mind. "You stick by me. We're a team, an unbeatable team. This whole countryside is ours for the taking!"

He gobbled up a small yellow hedgehopper who was sitting on a wooden post and instantly spit it out.

"Spicy. Phooey."

I looked back to see the yellow bug staggering about trying to figure out what had just happened.

All of a sudden we veered off the main road and ran up a steep hill. By the time we reached the top, I was puffing and had to sit down.

There were loads of people there. Flying kites. Large kites. The largest I had ever seen.

Taxi was hopping around thrilled out of his

mind. But then as other dogs started to draw closer, Taxi got a little peeved.

"Tell them to go away," he ordered.

But I didn't.

A black Lab trotted toward us and pushed Taxi aside.

"Howdy," the black Labrador said.

"Hang gliders," he explained, looking at all the overlarge kites.

"We *knew* that," Taxi said grumpily.

"They're *very* dangerous," the black Lab added. "Wait till you see what they do."

I felt my tail wagging a mile a minute from sheer excitement. Other dogs started to cluster around as we pushed closer to the crowd.

Five young men were lined up near the edge of the cliff, each holding on to a colorful glider.

Then off they ran, stepping into thin air. The crowd gasped as they floated off into the sky.

I pushed my way through the forest of legs until I was right there at the edge, looking out at the gliders, which seemed like a handful of bright confetti sprinkled against the dark-blue sky.

The gliders turned and swooped down toward us. Some people squealed and scattered.

I stood my ground. And was proud I had.

The gliders circled the crest of the hill while the crowd applauded and yelled.

I looked around for Taxi, hoping he wasn't missing this. But I couldn't see him anywhere. Was he sulking because I wouldn't tell the dogs to scram? Or was he just in one of his peculiar moods?

Ha! Lecturing me about being worldly, about meeting life halfway, when he was probably off picking on a grasshopper or terrorizing an otter.

On the next swoop, I looked up, blinked real hard, and looked again. And my heart stopped for a moment.

*Hanging on to one of the glider's backpacks . . . WAS TAXI!*

As they passed over our heads, Taxi *waved!*

"Is that the cat up there?" the black Lab asked.

"You know him?" another mutt asked.

I was so surprised that all I could do was nod.

The gliders soared through the open skies,

bursting through puffy clouds, dipping low over the fields, swooping dangerously close to the ocean, then gliding back again on the coattails of a breeze.

Finally they touched down.

I could see Taxi jumping onto the ground.

I started off toward him, barking my head off. Behind me came an entourage of other dogs.

"Weren't you scared?" I asked, panting from sheer excitement.

"Me, scared?" he bragged, strutting around in front of all the others. "Ninjas ought to be able to fly."

"Ninja? What's a ninja?" I heard one of the dogs ask.

"What is a NINJA?" Taxi asked, his eyes narrowing in that strange, exotic way. He flexed his muscles and started for the nearest tree.

Uh-oh, I thought. He was going to show off again.

Up the tree he scampered. Up and up until he was barely visible. I closed my eyes as he sailed off the uppermost branch. And disappeared from view.

"Where did he go?" the spaniel asked, scanning the horizon with all the other onlookers.

I could smell where he was but I kept my lip buttoned and waited until the other dogs got bored waiting and moved on. Then I pushed my way into the dense undergrowth. Farther and farther I pressed until I finally reached him.

Taxi and Sushi were trapped under a pile of tangled roots.

"Are they gone?" he asked.

"Yes."

I dug around, moving twigs and such, creating an opening through which he could squeeze out.

He was a mess. His tail was bent into strange angles. His whiskers were covered with filth, and his thin assistant looked no better.

"Did you watch, Huey? Did you see?"

"Did I see you take a nosedive into this thicket? Yes. And you should be delighted to know that I was the only one who did see you make a fool of yourself."

He gave me an astonished look.

"But I flew. I *felt* it! Lifting *up* and *up* and sort of floating alongside some birds?"

Now it was my turn to give him a look of astonishment.

"Excuse me for asking, but did you happen to fall on your head?"

"I would have flown more, except for Sushi."

He gave Sushi a good sound shake.

"Sushi got airsick."

What could I say? The cat was completely deluded. On an entirely different ozone level from everyone else's.

It took me a long time to bite all the burrs off him so he could walk on his own. It was dark before we started home.

Later that night I crept outside and watched as Taxi licked his wounds. I couldn't stand it. I had to say what I had to say.

"Taxi? Taking risks is one thing. Being reckless is quite another."

There was a long silence. I was certain that my good sense was finally penetrating his pulpy brain.

I looked at him. He looked at me.

Then he grinned and blew a raspberry.

# 9

Fred was writing a book. Maureen was decorating picture frames, mirrors, and lampshades with seashells and planning to sell them at the village fair.

Since I didn't have to worry about them too much, I started going everywhere Taxi suggested. Fred and Maureen never complained because we always came back.

The village wasn't too far away from where we lived. It was very small, with only one paved road and a few stores. Nothing to write home about. Except now everyone was beginning to spruce up the place for the fair.

Banners were being strung across the street announcing the event. Storekeepers were decorating their windows. Some were even washing their front doors.

A few animals were wandering around. The black Lab from the hang-gliding day. A couple of other pooches. A snapping turtle that you didn't *ever* want to get near and a pig called Rosie who sort of hung around the greengrocer's eating all the scraps.

Oh yeah, there was a goat. But he was very old and forgetful, and we had to reintroduce ourselves to him every time we went into town.

I followed my nose to the front of the grocery store. The screen door slapped open and shut as customers came and went. A little ham and cheese with a dollop of mustard was the dream lunch I was hoping for, but all I managed to get was half a doughnut. As I was finishing it, out of the store came an old cat. Ancient. With white whiskers, loose teeth, but kind, useless eyes.

"Did we meet? My name is Pete," he said.

"I'm Huey."

"I'm not scared of dogs. Come closer if you like."

I did as he continued to chat.

"I've been around so long now that the summers seem to be getting shorter and the winters much longer! It's my age, you know, I'm the oldest cat I know. The oldest in this

entire county. I noticed you once or twice before. You hang around with that strange cat."

"Taxi. His name is Taxi."

"Nice teeth."

"Yes, he does have good teeth . . ."

"No, I meant you."

"Why, thank you." I glanced about hoping that Taxi was watching me converse with Pete, like a bona fide country dog. But he was nowhere in sight.

"Well, I better go and check out the back of the store. That's my job. Making sure the mice don't take over." He wandered off. I got up and went to search for Taxi.

One sniff was all it took. I headed straight for the barbershop. I circled around the back and eased the door open with my nose.

And guess where he was. Tangled inside a mass of hanging *flypaper* in the back of the barbershop.

"GET ME DOWN!" Taxi yelled.

I started calling for help and finally the barber appeared.

"Well, I'll *be!*" he remarked, then lickety-splitted out of the room only to return a moment later with a *camera*.

"I'm gonna put this in the *Star Ledger*." He laughed as he took one photo after another of Taxi dangling in midair.

After he finished photographing Taxi, he cut him down. Once that cat's feet touched ground, he was O-F-F like a rocket, dragging the flypaper that was stuck to his feet right along after him.

I followed, turning once to bark a "thank you" at the barber. He didn't even notice me. He was too busy reloading his camera.

I caught up with Taxi behind the bank.

"GET THIS OFF ME!" he wailed.

But the instant I touched the paper, it stuck to me. And wouldn't you know it, within a few seconds I was completely tangled into the mass of flypaper *too*.

The more I struggled, the more snarled we became.

What a predicament.

If someone had told me a year ago that I'd be *trapped* in a tight ball with a *loony* cat, by *yards* of gluey paper, COVERED with zillions of dead flies, while an entire town was taking *PICTURES* of us, I would've called for the padded wagon right then and there!

I was never more humiliated in my life!

Every dog, cat, parakeet, turtle, worm, and ant had witnessed this ridiculous accident. We were the laughingstock of the entire county!

When some kind souls finally peeled off the last bit of paper, we ran toward the edge of town and didn't stop running until we reached home.

# 10

It was later that same night when something else happened that sort of changed the course of our lives.

It started with a noise. A sort of scuffling that came from somewhere under the roof.

I began barking my head off!

Fred and Maureen bolted from their room, pulling on their robes. Taxi, with Sushi in his mouth, didn't budge from the hanging plant where he had been asleep. But he watched with a beady eye.

"Something's up there," Fred said, getting a ladder. Maureen handed him a flashlight, and up he went.

"Be careful, darling," she cautioned.

Taxi stretched and yawned and rolled over in the ivy, totally unconcerned.

I was worried. What if it was one of those nasty raccoons? What if it lurched at Fred and knocked him off the ladder? What if he fell on Maureen?

Fred opened the hatch door in the ceiling and flashed the light inside.

"Can you see anything?" Maureen asked.

"It's a cat," Fred said.

A *what*?

"A what?" Taxi echoed my thoughts as he stood so quickly, he made the plant sway.

"It's terrified," Fred said. Maureen climbed up next to him while Taxi and I watched.

"Here, puss, puss. Oh, it's a girl. Isn't she beautiful?"

"She's wounded."

"Where?"

"Here, on her back."

They brought her down the ladder, placed her on the kitchen counter, and stood so I couldn't get a peek at what she looked like.

"She'll be all right with a little tender loving care," Fred said.

"She must be a stray," Maureen added. "At least I hope she is. Because then maybe we can keep her."

Another cat! Good gracious, I thought. Not another Taxi! One is quite enough in a basset hound's lifetime, thank you very much.

I looked up to see Taxi perched on a high shelf, staring down at the new cat, Sushi hanging from his mouth. His eyes were wide open. He was studying her as if she were some exotic germ or something.

Fred and Maureen finally moved away, so I could see her too.

She was beautiful. I mean really astonishing. All black with white tips on all four paws. And her eyes! They were huge. Almond shaped and very, very blue.

"We'll call her Boots," Maureen said. "Is that all right with you?" she asked Boots.

Boots, grateful for the water Fred had given her, arched her back, blinked her baby blues, and gave them both a long, appreciative purr.

"Hey, what about me?" I barked.

Fred laughed as he hoisted me up and plopped me on the countertop next to Boots.

Close up, she was even better-looking.

"H'lo," I gulped. And I think I may've blushed.

"Hello." She had a very nice voice. "I'm sorry if I upset you, barging in the way I did, but it was raining so hard, and I didn't know what else to do."

"No problem," I said. "Relax. Have some food. Want a Liver Treat? No, of course you don't. Well, if there's anything I can do for you, let me know. . . ."

I felt giddy. Silly, you know. It was the way she was looking at me that did it. A soft look, yet spellbinding.

She licked my face and purred.

"Thank you."

Suddenly Sushi dropped on her head. We looked up to see Taxi staring at both of us as he hung upside down from the curtain rod.

Boots stared back at him. He blinked. She blinked. Then she picked up Sushi and started to examine him.

In one second flat Taxi was there, nose to nose with her.

"Your string looks very chewed up," she said.

Taxi's eyes narrowed.

Oh no. I thought. Here we go again.

"*String? STRRIIIING!* This is Sushi! My own personal, private assistant and if *anyone* tries to mess with *him* . . . they are D-E-A-D!"

She cringed. She laid her ears back as he circled her menacingly, flexing his muscles, making weird hissing noises like a leaky radiator.

"Taxi, stop. You're frightening her," Maureen scolded. Taxi hightailed it out of the room. Maureen grabbed Boots, and Fred put me on the floor.

They took Boots into their bedroom for the night. Maybe they were afraid that Taxi might start a fight with her. Maybe they wanted to tend to her wound. Or maybe they felt she was something terribly special and didn't want to share her company.

They closed the door behind them.

I stood there for a moment.

I scratched at the door. But they didn't open it.

I trundled back to the living room and sniffed at the few scraps left in my dinner dish, circled my cushion a few times, then curled into it and started to relax.

Just before I drifted off, Taxi came in.

He found his ball of twine, which, on occasion he liked to bat around, and put it in the corner. Then he recovered a rubber mouse with a bell in it that he had never showed the least interest in and put that in the same corner.

He did the same with a squeaky rubber toy, his private stash of catnip, and a hat he wouldn't be caught dead wearing.

"What are you doing?" I asked him.

"Never trust a stray," he said. "They're scavengers. They'll take anything they can get. And what they can't get, they'll steal."

I couldn't imagine Boots wanting anything I owned. Except maybe my baseball hat with the sunglasses. And to tell you the truth, my heart wouldn't break if that suddenly disappeared.

But what interested me most was the possibility of Boots remaining with us. I wondered how it would alter our lives.

I was about to find out.

# 11

"You're Huey?" Boots purred the next morning as she came outside to join me.

I smiled as best I could and nodded.

"Howdy do," I offered as she made a circle around me.

Suddenly we were showered by a ton of leaves.

We looked up to see Taxi staring at us from a branch overhead.

"Hello, Taxi," she said.

"I am NINJA!" Taxi yelled. Then he let out a screech and went boinging from limb to limb, then boinged around the porch, on and off the barbecue, the railing, the hammock, the furniture. Like a Slinky toy gone loopy.

Boots blinked. Puzzled, she looked to me for an explanation.

"He's eccentric," I said. "Not your average, run-of-the-mill cat, if you know what I mean."

Taxi boinged down the path, scattering a bunch of frightened rabbits.

"He's not easy to get to know," I added, keeping my voice low. "But I assure you, he can be as brave as a lion, as energetic as a bagful of chimps, and as goofy as a dodo bird."

At that precise moment Taxi boinged back toward us.

He was up to some mischief. I could see it lurking behind those crossed green eyes of his. But before he had a chance to try anything, Maureen appeared.

"Come, Boots. We're going to the vet to have you checked out."

Vet.

That magic word.

ZIP, Taxi disappeared and didn't *reappear* until Fred and Maureen had left with Boots inside their station wagon.

It was a while before I found him sitting near the bay.

I loved the sound of sploshing waves. So I sat and watched Taxi boxing with the dragonflies hovering nearby.

"You think they're going to keep that cat?" Taxi asked.

"It seems very likely."

"They *have* a cat already."

He ducked as one of the dragonflies dive-bombed him.

"Some people have two cats, Taxi."

"I don't like this. It's been you and me for a long time. It won't be the same with her around."

"Why not?"

"A girl?" His eyes were incredulous. "She'll be a pain. She'll want to horn in on everything we do. And then she'll whine and complain and wanna do this or that . . . and you'll give in because you're soft in the head. And then I'll be left on my own."

"That won't happen."

"And that's not all. She'll try and become their favorite pet. And before you know it, both of us'll find ourselves in the pound."

"Come on, stop that."

"Look at us. We're misfits."

I peered at my reflection in the water. I didn't think I looked at all like a misfit.

I turned to tell Taxi so, but he had dashed

off to chase a turtle that slid into the bay before he could reach it.

"I'm not a misfit," I said.

"Yes you are. Do your ears fit your head? No. They need to be hemmed. Are your legs built to support your body . . . ?"

"Don't start, Taxi. Please."

"And as for me. Very few people understand me. Even I have trouble sometimes."

I bet!

We were strolling along one of the paths when we heard them returning. A second after the car door opened, Boots was by our side.

Wearing a collar just like Taxi and me.

"Can I join you?"

"NO!" Taxi spat. Boots crouched, then started to retreat. She looked hurt.

"Of course you can," I said quickly, and gave Taxi a stern look. He took Sushi and leaped into the nearest tree.

Boots hesitated.

"Come. I'll show you around," I offered.

"Thank you," she purred.

"Oh barf!" I heard Taxi exclaim.

We went through the woods and into a clearing.

"This is a hollowed-out tree trunk; I can't fit into it, but Taxi told me it's very cool inside."

"DON'T TOUCH MY SPIDERS!" came Taxi's voice from some branch overhead.

"He's referring to the spiders inside this tree trunk. Taxi considers this his sort of private . . . cafeteria."

"I only eat spiders by accident," Boots said.

"IS SHE TAKING ANY OF MY SPIDERS?" he called down.

"I wouldn't take anything of yours without asking," she called up.

"Oh sure," he said with a snort of disbelief.

"Come down and see, why don't you," I said.

But he wouldn't join us.

We moved on.

I was anxious to find out how she came to be inside our attic.

"I fell asleep in the back of a truck," she told me, "and when I woke up, I didn't know where I was. So I started to walk. I stayed for a while in a barn, but I had a fight with some raccoons."

"Is that where you were wounded?"

"Yes. Then it started to rain and I needed a

place to rest until I felt good enough to move on."

"Where do you come from? Were you ever a house cat?"

"When I was very young. A little boy found me with my mother and took me home with him. He was wonderful. We were never apart. But when the summer ended, they packed up the house, boarded the windows, and left. I could see the little boy crying as he waved good-bye to me from the back of the car. I didn't know what was happening. I waited and waited for them to come back for me. But they didn't."

Well, you live and learn.

I searched overhead, hoping that Taxi had heard this story. I could smell him nearby. But I couldn't see him.

"She's turning you against me," he said later, when we were alone.

"Snortswaggle," I declared. I hated to use such beastly language, but he was being his old impossible self.

"She is. You spent the entire day acting like some stupid *tour guide*, listening to her life story, and never *once* thought that maybe, just *maybe*, I wanted to take a ride on a raft or head into town or something. I could've been lying dead somewhere for all you cared."

Honestly. What could I say?

Suddenly he spun around and gave a hanging leaf a karate chop. Then he sprang onto a low-lying limb and was off, with Sushi dangling from his mouth.

He'll get over it, I thought.

# 12

I was wrong. He got worse.

"I don't want *her* food next to mine!" And with that he nosed Boots's bowl clear across the room and down the cellar steps, spilling food all over the place.

"Who did this?" Maureen asked when she returned.

Taxi put on an innocent face, swatting at a cricket, while Boots tagged along behind Maureen, trying to help her clean up by eating whatever she could.

As soon as Boots curled up in a corner to take a nap, Taxi swooped in and whipped the cushion out from under her.

"*This* is mine," he hissed.

"I'm sorry, I thought the one over there was yours."

"They're *all* mine! Everything in this place is mine. That table, that chair, the dustballs

under that sofa, the *air you breathe*, mine . . .
it's all mine! . . ."

Then he moved real close to her, eyeball to
eyeball.

"Why don't you take a long walk off a short
pier?" he snapped.

And did he use that cushion?

Of course not. He slept over doors, as he
always did.

When Boots was resting on Maureen's lap,
being stroked and petted, Taxi would dash
away, returning a moment later to deposit
two dead crickets and a half-eaten grasshopper at Maureen's feet.

Maureen was too busy with Boots to notice.

"What a beautiful puss-puss," she said.

Taxi was outraged. Pacing back and forth,
he spouted.

"I keep this place free of bugs and what do I
get? A simple 'thank you'? No. All she wants
to do is carry that mangy cat around, talking
baby talk to her. Makes me want to puke!
ICK!"

I suppose it got to be too much for him,
because he leaped onto the countertop and *bit*
Boots's tail.

Can you believe it?

Boots screamed, Maureen yelled, and Taxi, a little surprised at himself, skidded across the counter, upsetting a glass, dove out the open door and shot up the first tree he came to.

I ran outside to have some words with him.

After all, he was still my pet, and his behavior was appalling!

"Your behavior is shocking!" I said sternly.

"Keep out of this, Porkbrains. I know what I'm doing."

"No you don't!"

"She thinks she can move in here and take over. Well, not without a fight."

Maureen appeared and sat on the stoop next to me.

"Hello, Huey. What a good dog."

I could see Boots peering through the screen at us.

"I'm a little worried. Do you think Taxi might be a bit jealous of Boots?"

"A *bit* jealous! HA!" I said, only it came out half grumble, half howl.

"I hate to see him so unhappy."

"He'll live," I answered. She reached over

and began to scratch behind my ears.

"I don't want him to be mean to Boots."

"Well, if he is, send him back to the pound." Maybe she didn't understand me, but Taxi sure did. He pushed a fat acorn off the branch above me that bonked me on the nose.

"I'd be happy to make a fuss over him too, but he hates to be petted," Maureen said. "But you don't, do you? Does this feel good?" she asked, giving my back a scratch.

You bet. Only . . . a little to the right. Yeah.

"I hope Taxi doesn't become one of those neurotic cats," she added.

"*Become* one! They don't *come* more neurotic than Taxi."

Another acorn beaned me on the head.

"If only you could talk, Huey, I bet you'd have all the right answers. Wouldn't you?"

"I hate to sound immodest, but yes, I would."

"I think I'm going to be sick," Taxi said from above me.

Maureen patted me on the head and kissed my nose, then went inside.

Taxi hopped down and sat next to me.

"See how she's turning everyone against

me? She's cast a spell over all of you!"

"A spell?"

His eyes went all quirky.

"She's tried it with me. Staring me in the eyes until I could see myself in there. Making my legs go weak. Ninja knows. Ninja will not be tricked. Come, Sushi."

He grabbed his string and marched off into the dark.

Boots came outside and sat next to me.

"He hates me, doesn't he?"

"No. He needs more time. That's all. Quiet time with no one else around. So he can get to know you better."

I was stricken right there and then with an idea.

"Come," I said to her.

She followed me down to the bay, where we found Taxi seated on the raft, Sushi coiled in repose next to him. His eyes widened when he saw us approaching.

Onto the raft we went.

"Watch out," he yelled. "You want to capsize us? Get off! This raft only takes three."

"But we *are* only three," Boots purred.

"We're *four!*" He said, holding up Sushi.

"And Sushi doesn't weigh as much as you do."

While he was carrying on, I undid the rope and cast us adrift.

Yes, I did. How's *that* for nerve?

And when they both turned and saw what I had done, the expression on their faces was worth the risk I had taken.

# 13

My plan was to drift across to the other side. Visit some cows. Have a little adventure in the daylight and end up with all of us being the best of friends.

Taxi had spent so much of his time hatching plans to make her feel unwelcome that he couldn't appreciate her finer qualities.

Like her sense of humor.

The second night she was with us, she dragged an old bootlace out of the closet and began hopping around the living room, doing a marvelous imitation of Taxi playing with Sushi. Batting it around. Pouncing on it. Boinging around with the bootlace in her mouth.

My sides almost split, I was laughing so hard.

Did Taxi see it?

Yes! And the expression on his face made

me laugh even harder. It was a scream!

But I'm digressing.

Here we were on a raft, where I watched as my well-intentioned plan suddenly turned *drastically* sour!

What I hadn't considered was the tide.

The raft began swirling and bouncing over the waves, hurtling us toward the mouth of the bay and, beyond that, the open sea.

I gasped.

Boots, a little shocked at what I had done, watched the landscape whizzing past us.

Taxi gave me a look as if I had entirely lost touch with my common sense. Then he took charge.

"Okay. Nobody panic. Blimpo? Jump over the side. Grab the rope and pull us in."

"But the water's moving too swiftly. I'll drown."

"You got us into this and now you can get us out."

"But look at the waves. They're monstrous!"

You know what that miserable cat did? He bit me on my butt.

*YEOCH!*

Over the side I hopped, where I began

paddling like crazy. The rope was in my mouth.

Logs raced past my head as I swam toward the jetty. A horseshoe crab spun past my nose. Branches and old tin cans bobbed past my ears. I was beginning to lose ground. The tide was overpowering.

"To the right!" Taxi commanded.

"No," Boots called, "swim toward that tree. That's where the tide is taking you."

"The jetty," Taxi called. "Swim for the jetty!"

"The tree. I have an idea," she added.

The tree seemed easier. So while they continued to argue, I headed for the weeping willow.

As soon as we drew close enough, Boots leaped onto my head and from there sprang for one of the branches. As quick as lightning, she scooted to the thin end of the branch and forced it down, so that it hung into the water and stopped the raft.

I let go of the rope and paddled for shore.

I shook the water off as Taxi leaped onto the bank beside me. I could see the raft sailing away. Out of sight, around the next bend.

"Thank you, Boots," I said. "You saved our

lives. And such quick thinking."

She smiled and licked my face.

"You learn an awful lot when you've been on your own."

She turned her baby blues on Taxi.

"I'm glad we're all safe."

He seemed mesmerized for a moment. Sort of hypnotized by her look. Then he stepped back, fell over a root, rose quickly, and put on one of his more menacing looks.

"You didn't save anyone, sister. Ninja needs no one to save him."

She kept staring at him.

"Butting into what doesn't concern you?" Taxi continued in his menacing tone. "You think I didn't know how to get us back safely? Well, I did! We didn't need you telling us what to do. We've been getting along just *fine* without you. And we'll get along even *better* when you leave!"

She looked so hurt.

"Taxi," I scolded.

"Don't worry," Taxi said. "She's not going anywhere. Strays are like ticks. You have to bite them *real* hard to make them let go."

Stung, she backed away and started to

leave, when suddenly she spun around, rushed at Taxi, and nipped his tail.

He was so startled that he fell back, *squish*, right on top of Sushi.

Then she ran off.

"Boots," I called.

"She bit me." He was positively rattled.

"Not hard enough," I answered as I started off to see where she had gone.

"She's probably eating my spiders!" he yelled.

"She *hates* spiders!"

"That's what they all say, then as soon as you check out your supply, you find half-eaten ones, ones with the middles poked in, or all the crunchy ones gone!"

He was simply impossible!

A thoroughly *maddening* cat!

## 14

She had disappeared all right. And can you blame her?

Taxi finally had what he wanted: a one-cat household.

Yet somehow, things would not go back to normal.

First off, the Waltons missed her terribly. They went out looking for her. Calling and calling. Finally, with very sad faces, they left her food outside the door, in hopes that she would return.

But she didn't.

A few mice and several hundred ants enjoyed the Chicken Giblet Holiday Surprise Dinner.

Maureen left Boots's cushion in the same spot, and near it all her toys.

I missed her too. And it was strange to think that I was ever worried about having a

newcomer living with us. It had taken only one look in her eyes and *click*, we had hit it right off. As if we had been friends all our lives.

I think it would be fair to say that although she had been with us for such a short time, she'd had a resounding effect on all of us.

And how was Taxi behaving?

He couldn't believe that she was gone. He refused to admit that just about everything he had said about her was *wrong*.

"She's around here somewhere," Taxi insisted. "Believe me, I know her kind."

"She isn't, Taxi. I smelled every square inch of this area and I'm telling you . . . "

"SHHH. Listen!" Taxi perked up. "You hear that?"

I sniffed the air, but the breeze was blowing the wrong way. Taxi stayed close to the ground like a cobra, winding his way toward some low-lying bushes. He rose up on his haunches screeching:

"HERE SHE IS!"

Suddenly his screech turned into a horrifying *YOWL* that blended with another *YOWL*.

Dust flew. Leaves scattered. And out from the bushes lurched a thoroughly nasty-looking creature, snarling, grunting, and snapping its teeth. Before I could catch a proper look, it dove into the burrowed-out root of a tree.

Taxi sat on the ground looking dazed.

"What was *that*?"

"A weasel!"

"A *what*?"

"A weasel!"

"That was the *ugliest* thing . . . a weasel? *ECHT!*"

He dusted off Sushi and headed down the road.

We ventured to the top of the hill where Taxi had gone hang gliding. From there we had a view of the entire countryside.

It was beautiful.

Taxi's eyes were scanning the trees. And bushes. At every shadow his eyes would narrow. The slightest movement and his head would swivel around, his ears turning into little radar receptors.

He couldn't fool me.

Not one bit.

He was searching for Boots.

"Maybe tomorrow we should head into town," I offered.

He gave me a long look, then nodded.

"Yes. Tomorrow we'd better check out the town."

# 15

The road leading into town was jam-packed with cars and pickup trucks and kids on bikes.

It looked like a large carnival. There were rides. Hot dogs. Popcorn. Games kids were playing and lots of dogs and cats.

Fred and Maureen arrived before we did. All the frames and mirrors she had decorated so beautifully were displayed on one of the stands. I loped over and gave her a hello. She bent down and scratched my ears.

I could see Taxi marching on ahead, peering left and right, as if he were watching a Ping-Pong game. I broke away from Maureen and Fred and joined him.

For a while we strolled along, looking at the vendors, kids playing games, and people walking around carrying tiny goldfish in plastic bags.

We passed the black Lab eating cotton

candy he stole from a baby. Next to him was an Irish setter licking a puddle of ice cream on the sidewalk.

"Want some?" the setter asked.

"Why, thank you," I said, and was about to take a lick when Taxi pulled me away.

"Later," he snapped.

"But it won't be there later."

"Tough toots," was all he said.

As soon as we turned the next corner, we saw them. Boots with another cat. A good-looking cat, too. They were having fun chasing a wind-up butterfly a kid was playing with on the street.

The expression on Taxi's face was worth a zillion, trillion, gadzillion Liver Treats.

He was absolutely, positively FLABBER-GASTED.

"Who's she with? Who is that cat? What is she doing?" he stammered.

Boots turned to us for a moment and sent me a friendly smile. She refused to give Taxi even the merest nod.

"Did you see that? She looked straight through me, as if I weren't here," Taxi said, stunned.

"Can you blame her after what you said to her? Anyway, she's having fun. Look."

"With *that* CAT? How could she? *ECCHHH!* Look at his ears! And his *whiskers!* Where does he live? Inside a lawn mower?"

The cat looked perfectly all right to me. And so did Boots, which seemed to irk Taxi even more.

Two small kids strolled close to us. Both were carrying hot dogs. I was desperate for one itsy-bitsy nibble.

I edged closer, opened my mouth and was inches away from the hot dog when . . . *YOUCH!*

"What are you *doing?*" Taxi demanded. He yanked me away by my ear, then dragged me around the corner.

"Have you gone stark raving mad?" I asked him.

"She shouldn't be hanging around that cat. He's no good. Go tell her."

I looked at him real hard. I couldn't believe my ears.

"I can't tell her anything like that."

His face twisted. And he nipped my foot.

"WOOOooOooooo."

107

"Oh quiet. I hardly touched you," he said as he peered around the corner.

"She's gone."

He leaped onto my back and looked both ways.

"You stay here! If you see them coming, let out a bark. One of your WOOooOOOoOOoo's."

"Who's *them*?"

He gave my nose a tweak.

"Who do you think, Porkbrains? Boots and that ratty cat she's with."

He climbed onto a gridwork of steel beams. Up and up he climbed.

No sooner had he disappeared over the top than the beams started to move. Music spilled out from underneath all the steel.

We had been standing behind a carnival ride! I ran around the front and looked up, trying to spot Taxi.

Some people began to point at one of the cars.

There he was! Spread-eagled against the back of a bright-red car that was spinning and swirling over a bumpy track. Taxi's eyes were like saucers. His ears were sticking straight up and his tail was flattened against the back of the seat.

Boots came running too, her new friend by her side, and both of them as alarmed as I was.

"WOooooOooooOooo" was all I could say.

The people rushed over to the operator of the ride to make him stop it. They pointed in Taxi's direction. The operator peered out of his box, saw Taxi, and quickly pulled on the brakes.

The ride jerked to a stop so fast that Taxi went sailing out of the car and landed on a carousel horse.

We all raced over to see if he was all right.

"Are you all right?" Boots asked. The male cat she was with was laughing. He apparently thought the whole thing was very amusing.

"I'm *fine!* As if you care," he snarled.

"Of course I do. You know that," she said with great sincerity.

He stared into her large, soft eyes. Blinked. And then gulped.

"Get down off that thing," the carousel man yelled, and tossed a stone at him.

Boots's friend roared with laughter.

Taxi's eyes narrowed. He let out one of his

awesome jungle screeches and began to show off by leaping from beam to beam.

I knew what that meant. So I closed my eyes and cringed, waiting for disaster to strike.

But this time it was different. Taxi seemed positively inspired.

He did cartwheels over painted wooden animals. Ran up the side of the carousel and vaulted from pillar to post.

People clustered around to watch the ninja warrior go through his routine. Even the man who had just yelled at him came out and stared at his antics in wonder.

All the while he did this, Taxi kept sneaking peeks at Boots. Wanting to see her reaction. Wanting to impress her. Maybe this was his way of apologizing to her for his nasty behavior.

When he finally stopped, people applauded.

"That was splendid," I said, running over to him.

But Taxi was too busy staring at Boots to answer me. He had a funny look on his face. Soft and kind of goofy.

"That was remarkable," Boots said to him.

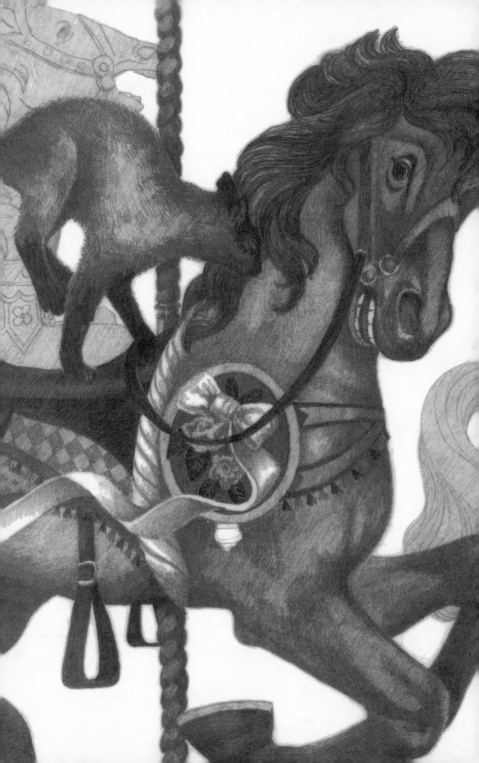

Instead of saying "Gee, thanks," or something like that, he quickly spun around and strutted off.

Confused, Boots waited a moment and then went off in the opposite direction, alone.

I ran to catch up with her. I wanted to know what was what. Where she was living.

"With Pete," she answered.

"You mean at the grocery store?" I was thrilled.

"He needed help. I'll stay until winter. Then I'll try and find another home." She smiled at me. "How have you been, Huey?"

"It isn't the same without you," I said.

"I miss you too," she confessed. With a sad look, she licked my nose and sped away.

I found Taxi sitting under a tree, grooming himself. He looked up, surprised to see I was alone.

"Where is she?"

"She isn't coming home."

He looked beyond me again.

"Of course she is."

"No, she's not. Why would she want to?"

He refused to believe me and sat smack in the middle of the road and waited.

I sat with him.

And sat.

And waited. And waited.

Lights were switched off. Tents came down. Trucks drove off with the rides.

And before very long it was only Taxi and I sitting in the middle of a big empty plot of land.

The only other creature sharing the night with us was some owl, hooting under the eaves of an old barn.

# 16

That little episode really started him thinking, I guess, because he grew listless and mostly stayed draped over doors, looking more like a limp bathroom mat than a respectable ninja warrior.

Moths, crickets, beetles, centipedes, flies, mosquitoes, and wasps came and went as they pleased. Taxi couldn't care less.

There was a penny frog who took up residence in the kitchen, but he had a limited appetite. His preference was for gnats and fireflies.

So I was left with the undignified job of telling off several species of bugs. And some of them were *extremely* rude.

"Scram," I said to a caterpillar. "Out! Out!"

"Keep your pants on," the snooty caterpillar yelled back. "I'm moving as fast as I can."

"For someone with so many legs, you're not doing too well."

I looked up to see if Taxi was watching. He wasn't.

"Okay, fellas, beat it." I slapped at the lampshade, scattering the moths who were clustered there. But moments later they were back, in exactly the same spots as before.

I had no idea what a mammoth job it was to debug a house.

"How could she go off with that lopsided bug-eyed cat with those needly whiskers?" Taxi asked once.

"If you're so worried, why don't *you* ask her," I huffed.

"I'm not *worried*. I'm being *curious*. That's what cats are best at, in case you didn't know."

Then he began leaving Sushi everywhere.

I was forever tripping over that dumb string. Once I found it hanging over the garbage-can lid. Another time I had to wrestle it away from a pack rat who was trying to stuff it into a hole in the wall.

No, nothing would ever be the same again, it seemed.

All of us were missing Boots. Even Taxi.

Her cushion was still where Maureen and Fred had left it. Her toys too. But now her food dish was side by side with Taxi's bowls.

He didn't know it, but I saw him nose it there when he thought I was fast asleep.

It had been impossible to go outside since the day of the fair. Rain came down in buckets. Day and night. An endless deluge.

So we stayed in, staring out through the rain-spattered doors.

Fred and Maureen started to notice Taxi's unusual behavior. They offered him some treats, but he spurned everything. When Maureen shook out Boots's pillow and by accident left it on a shelf, Taxi dragged it back to its original space.

I couldn't even try to engage him in a conversation. He was thinking about Boots.

Maybe he was remembering how badly he had treated her. How wrong he had been about her from the start. Jealous, even, that she had found another cat to keep company with.

Oh yes, he was missing her too.

Late one night, I found him in front of the full-length mirror, batting the bootlace that Boots had played with. The one she had pretended was Sushi.

I didn't want him to see me watching him, so I stayed low to the floor and kept very still.

He pranced and danced and shook the bootlace about. Then he sat down and groomed it. After that, he placed it gently next to Sushi.

He sighed and stared at himself in the mirror.

I felt a very tender spot for him. The poor fool had invented himself, ninja warrior and all, but didn't have a clue about how to behave like a normal cat.

Being locked inside with a depressed cat is not my idea of fun, I can tell you, so when the rain finally stopped, both of us made a bee-line for the door.

"I think we should take a trip to town," he said.

"Absolutely," I agreed.

He seemed rather nervous, stopping every once in a while to groom himself.

Once he even held up Sushi for me to look at.

"Do you like the way I parted his hair?" he asked.

I looked from the string to Taxi and back to the string.

Once a nutcase, always a nutcase, I suppose.

I could see the town only minutes away and wondered how long it would take before he found out where Boots was.

Well, let me suggest that if you *ever* have a secret, *never* confide in a cocker spaniel. They have strawberry Jell-O for brains. It's yakkity, yakkity, yak.

"Hi, Huey. Hi Taxi. That was some show you put on the other night. Those tricks you did at the fair? I was sure you must've been a circus cat or something, but Boots said you weren't."

"Boots?" Taxi asked. "Have you seen her? Where is she?"

"I'm not supposed to say."

Taxi was suddenly nose to nose with the spaniel.

"Listen, Dragonbreath, tell me where she is or . . ."

"I can't! You're not supposed to know that she's living in the back of the grocery store."

See? Jell-O for brains!

By the time I scooted around the back of the grocery store, Taxi was already there, perched atop the rain barrel, peering in through the grimy window.

I nosed the creaky door open, just enough for me to peek in too. And there she was. As beautiful as ever. Grooming herself inside a small circle of sunlight. Her black fur was so shiny, her eyes so sparkling.

"Is she alone?" he asked.

She looked up at the sound of his voice and impaled Taxi with a look. He gulped, spun around too fast, and nearly pitched into the barrel of rainwater.

"Go inside and tell her she should stop acting stupid and come home. Tell her Fred and Maureen are sick with worry . . . something dramatic like that."

"You go tell her."

His eyes grew wide. He bared his teeth. His ears were practically steaming.

Wanting to avoid bloodshed, I went in.

Boots was terribly pleased to see me. And I her.

"Fred and Maureen want you back home. They're very upset that you left."

"I can't go back there, Huey, and you know why I can't."

"You do as you're told," Taxi yelled from the door.

"I'm grown up and entirely responsible for myself," she said, walking straight over to him.

"I'm not afraid of your puffing and stomping and showing off anymore. You're a big bully, Taxi, and bullies can become terrible bores. I would much rather face my chances living in the outside world than live in a home where someone doesn't know what strength there is in a little kindness."

Taxi didn't know what to do. He stared hard at her for a moment, then spun around and dove outside, where for some demented reason he chased Rosie the pig all the way up Main Street.

I was delighted that she had told him off. It was about time.

I bid her good-bye and tried to find him.

He was heading home, grumbling.

I couldn't even begin to have a conversation with him.

All he wanted to do was grumble.

Grumble, grumble, grumble.

He swiped at a chipmunk sharing the path with us.

"Cut that out!" The chipmunk snapped. "My ancestors lived here way before you moved into the neighborhood. Who do you think you are, anyway?"

"I'm Ninja the Great, you little squirt. Now get lost before I make a chipmunk burger out of you."

"Taxi!" I yelled.

"Keep out of this. I know how to handle chipmunks."

"Pardon me for saying this, but I don't think you do. Nor do you know how to behave with those who care about you," I said.

He was silent. His eyes shifted sideways to give me a look.

"I know you have a deeply tender side."

"Are you saying I'm mushy?"

"No! I'm saying you have great tenderness which *very* few of us have had the pleasure of seeing. Especially Boots. All you ever do is shout at her. Don't you see that? All you need to do is show her the tender part."

"Yeah? Well." He hemmed and hawed and

finally said, "I don't have to prove anything to Sushi. Sushi knows . . ."

Suddenly he looked around, panic-stricken. "Sushi! Where's Sushi?!"

# 17

He raced back to town, me running as fast as I could, and found Sushi near the rain barrel, half hanging out of the water. Taxi grabbed his string and paused.

We could hear some noise coming from the back of the store and decided to take a look.

It was Boots with old Pete, who was swinging on one of the lower branches of red maple. Not showing off. Pete was too old and arthritic to be doing anything like that.

Taxi stood at the side, studying Boots with mad green eyes. I could tell he was plotting what to do next.

Suddenly he dropped Sushi at my feet and ran up the tree and spoke to Pete.

"When you leap, your back should be straight," he said. Then, making sure Boots was watching, he demonstrated his fabulous technique. From limb to limb he sailed.

If I could've applauded, I would've.

Boots leaped onto a branch and executed a few excellent leaps and spins and pirouettes in midair, then *sprang* onto the roof of the barn.

"It's better to bend your forelegs when you land," she suggested.

Now it was Taxi's turn to be surprised. The look on his face was pure astonishment.

He skittered across the roof and sailed through the air, catching onto a branch of the farthest tree.

Boots, shooting him a smile, tore across the roof and flew over the branch where Taxi was seated and onto the farthest building.

Then they began to sort of leapfrog over each other, obviously having loads of fun. Showing off to each other as only cats can do.

Watching with me was Pete, the spaniel, an army of ants, a couple of squirrels, and Rosie, who had developed an appetite after her run up Main Street and was devouring garbage nearby.

Soon Taxi and Boots were zipping around the rooftop, batting a pine cone around. We were all having a whale of a time when the grocer suddenly started banging on a tin pot.

"It's suppertime," Pete said. "Come along, Boots. Excuse us," he said to me. "We don't want to get locked out." He ran off.

I looked up just in time to see Boots scamper down the tree and head for the door right behind Pete. She turned and gave me an apologetic look just before the grocer shut the door.

Taxi stood outside and stared at the closed door.

"I guess that's it for tonight," I said.

He didn't answer me. He just stood there.

I wanted to cheer him up, so I threw the pine cone straight at him.

"Catch," I said.

It hit him in the head. *Bonk.*

But he didn't do a thing.

# 18

Taxi's behavior became more and more bizarre.

Sighing, pacing, irritable, he started talking to himself and thrashing Sushi around. He wouldn't eat, no matter what Maureen or Fred gave him. All Taxi wanted was to go into town.

He was driving me bananas!

And every time we went into town, there Boots would be, going about her business. She had an entirely different life and seemed happy and contented.

It nearly drove Taxi to distraction.

He would plan it so they would bump into each other. And when they did . . . forget it.

They would stand stock-still. Transfixed! As if they had both turned into little cat statues. And they'd stare into each other's eyes. Unable to speak.

Afterward he would march home, carrying on like some banshee with his tail on fire.

Pacing, grumbling, unable to speak or eat, just waiting to start the whole sorry mess all over again.

I suppose I finally realized the truth before Taxi did.

He was in love.

It was as clear as the nose on my face.

And if you've ever seen the nose on a basset hound, you'll realize that's about as *clear* as you can get!

Yes, he was in love. Pierced through the heart with one of Cupid's arrows.

And you know something else?

Boots was in the same state.

Now isn't that something? Both of them in love and neither one capable of breaking the ice.

Dogs are much more open about romance. They tear around yelping and drooling, and end up, sometimes, making a downright nuisance of themselves.

Cats are more private.

That's how I perceived this whole thing.

What I did know was that something *had* to be done.

Someone had to step in and help them out. Someone worthy and wise. Someone sensitive and cunning. Someone rather exceptional.

I hate to sound immodest, but I seemed to fit the bill, so I put my superior brain into gear and tried to crank out a brilliant idea.

Well, at this point, even a mediocre idea would be better than no idea at all.

So that night, as Taxi lay snoring and grumbling, completely tangled up in his string, I snuck out and went into town on my own.

That's right. On my own.

I know. I'm rather impressed myself.

I found Pete out back giving himself a good scratch.

"Too much pride can be a terrible curse." That's how I started the discussion. It caught his attention right off.

He confided that Boots had been suffering almost as much. Crying herself to sleep, then pretending she was fine as soon as Taxi showed up.

I outlined the plan I had hatched, and asked for his help. It was based on a strong hunch that Taxi would set his pride aside if he thought there might be a chance of losing Boots *forever*.

But I mustn't jump ahead of myself.

Pete helped me round out my plan, and then we went over each step. Unfortunately, as we got toward the end, Pete had already forgotten the beginning.

By the time we were finished, I had to race home to be in time for my early-morning dip in the bay with Fred and Maureen.

"Look at Taxi. Do you think he's sick?" Fred observed.

"He's been acting like that ever since Boots went away," Maureen added.

I paddled around them and took a peek.

Taxi was sitting on a rock with a leaf on his head. It had fallen from a nearby tree. Looked at from this angle, he seemed to be wearing a very peculiar hat.

I giggled to myself. Not because he looked especially silly, which he did, but because I was nervous. My plan *had* to work!

I shook off the water and trundled over to Taxi while Fred and Maureen dried off.

As I drew closer, I could hear a squeaky, irate voice. A young chipmunk, snagged under one of Taxi's paws, was desperately trying to get away.

"Get me outta here," it was screeching. Taxi

didn't even seem to notice it was there.

I moved Taxi's leg and the chipmunk freed himself.

"You cross-eyed *clunk*!" He yelled up at Taxi, then kicked dirt at him before scurrying off.

"Well," I said. "I heard some troubling news."

He didn't react. I swallowed real hard. Being rather new to this game of intrigue, I was afraid I wouldn't act out my part effectively.

"It looks as if Boots will be moving away real soon."

That got his attention.

"Some farmers are taking her away today. Pete said they were going to keep her locked up in their barn so she could keep the mice under control."

Yep. His eyes were getting wider as he listened. I took another gulp and made my eyes look real, *real* sad.

"To think of someone of Boots's quality and spirit forced to do something so . . . *demeaning*!"

His eyes started to twitch.

"They'll probably marry her off to that cat. You remember the one she was with at the fair? Personally I thought he was attractive as cats go, but . . ."

I didn't get a chance to finish my sentence. To a stranger passing by, it may've appeared as if I had lit a firecracker under that poor cat, because he took off like a rocket.

As I raced along behind him, I began to feel butterflies inside my stomach.

It was important for Pete to get Boots into the truck that delivered produce to the store each week. But what if he couldn't convince Boots to get into the truck? What if the produce truck never showed up? What if it had a flat tire? What if Pete forgot everything I had told him?

The "what-ifs" *always* drive me crazy.

But I recalled what Taxi had said to me once: Sometimes you have to go out and meet life halfway. And that's what I was doing.

Taxi charged into town like a tiger.

"There's the truck," I yelped.

It was parked in front of the grocery store. In two seconds flat Taxi was on the hood, looking in through the windshield.

Boots, sitting in the front seat, was stunned to see him.

"You can't go! Get out of there! You'll ruin your life! Don't go! Please. I beg you," Taxi pleaded.

She looked completely amazed as she rose on her back legs and pressed her nose against the window.

"What are you talking about?"

He melted. Captivated by her look.

"You can't go away. You can't marry that . . . mangy no-good cat. You deserve better. Please, listen to me."

He started to scrabble at the window, trying to get in.

I barked.

Out came the farmer, who threw some empty crates into the back and opened the door.

Taxi let out one of his ninja screams, and the surprised farmer quickly backed away. Boots jumped out of the front seat into some bushes, with us following behind.

She licked my face, then looked up as Taxi drew closer. He hung his head low, slowly inching closer to her.

"I acted like a real jerk and I'm sorry. Very sorry," he finally said.

His voice was tender and shaky. He held up his battered string.

"Sushi wants you to know that he misses you very much."

Boots smiled and licked Sushi.

Then she and Taxi gazed at each other for a long time.

I cleared my throat, which broke the spell.

"Please come home," Taxi said. "Sushi would like that very much . . . ?"

"And what about you?" she asked, her voice quivering.

He swallowed hard. This was very difficult.

"Please? Life is not happy . . . without you."

I could feel love radiating from each of them and felt tears welling up in my eyes. I can't help it. I'm an emotional slob. I cry at weddings, happy endings, and pictures of baby pandas.

"You can give me a swift kick in the butt if it would make you feel any better," he offered.

I certainly wanted to give him a swift kick. But my good taste and high breeding made me refrain from doing so.

They arched their backs, closed their eyes, and pressed against each other's sides. Both of them purring, their tails sticking up like banners, the tips making tiny flicking motions. I was so ecstatic that I couldn't contain myself.

I boinged around Main Street like some absolute idiot. Then I chased Rosie up Main Street. Neither one of us trotted very fast. But it did cause a few people to step out of their stores and give us both a smile.

When I rejoined Taxi and Boots, I gave them each a great, big slurpy kiss. And I gave one to Sushi too.

I was so happy that I was beginning to have a jawache from smiling so much.

But when I stopped, my whole face went sort of *plop*. It's awfully hard for basset hounds to smile, because everything has to curl up to create a smile, when in truth everything on a basset hound's face tends to slump down.

After a time we started down the road toward home, me on one side of Boots and Taxi on the other.

"I don't know who told you that story, but I wasn't going off with the farmer."

Taxi moved closer to her.

"It doesn't matter. You're with us forever. That's all I care about."

They shared a smile.

Maureen and Fred were going to be thrilled to see us.

As we headed up a rise, we could see some men, way off in the distance, blowing up a magnificent hot-air balloon.

"Have you ever been in one of those?" Taxi asked.

"Me? Never," I said.

"I haven't either. Have you?" Boots asked of Taxi.

"No."

He turned suddenly and gave me a grin.

"Maybe we should check it out later on." A twinkle glowed in his demented green eyes.

Uh-oh. I thought. Here we go again.

For some reason I couldn't quite picture the four of us, including Sushi, getting into a hot-air balloon.

No.

Impossible.

Or was it?

But I mustn't digress.

*That's* another story altogether.

MARION COUNTY PUBLIC LIBRARY
321 MONROE ST.
FAIRMONT, W. VA. 26554

DATE DUE

Marion County Public Library

1000034631

Copy 2